THE SPY FIVE
OPERATION
FOWL PLAY

by **Spencer Strange**

with

Andrea Menotti *words*

and

Kelly Kennedy *pictures*

Scholastic Inc.

New York Toronto London Auckland Sydney
Mexico City New Delhi Hong Kong Buenos Aires

Visit the Spy Five web site at
www.scholastic.com/spyfive!

Your new password is:

fowlplay

Use this password
to access a new
game!

ISBN 0-439-70349-2

Copyright © 2004 by Scholastic Inc.

Design: Julie Mullarkey Gnoy

12 11 10 9 8 7 6 5 4 3 2 1   4 5 6 7 8 9/0

Printed in the U.S.A.

First printing, October 2004

CHAPTERS

CHAPTER 1
CLARENCE DISCOVERS A UHO

Chicken nugget day is always a special day at lunch, because nuggets are even *more* popular than Tater Tots for chucking across the room. Especially with ketchup on them.

But that Wednesday was even more special than most, because *that* was the day that Clarence found an Unidentified Hard Object inside his nugget.

"GROOOOSSSSSS!"

Clarence gagged, so loud you could even hear him where Julian and I were sitting, over at the next table.

By the time we were on the scene, a big crowd of kids had gathered around to look at the UHO, which was in a blob of spat-out nugget on Clarence's tray.

It was pretty gross, especially considering I'd just eaten the nuggets myself.

UHO

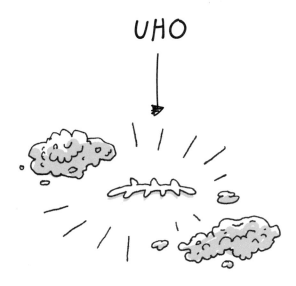

"You could *sue* for that," one of the kids said.

"Yeah, sue!" another kid said. "I heard this lady got like ten million dollars 'cause she found a finger in her root beer can."

"I heard it was a *rat*," someone else said.

"A whole rat?" Julian asked. "It fit inside the can?"

What's worse? — YUCK!

"People!" Clarence shouted. "I'm already sick *enough*."

"What's going on here?" someone asked.

It was Ursula, pushing through to the front of the crowd.

"Clarence found that thing inside his nugget," I said. "What do you think it is?"

Ursula looked down at it, wrinkling her nose.

"Maybe it's a rat part?" Julian said. "'Cause that could be worth ten million..."

"Easy, tiger," Ursula said. "It's probably just a chicken bone."

But then she looked a little closer, wrinkling her nose even more.

"But then again, you never know with *this* school," she said.

"Give it to the cafeteria ladies!" someone said. "Ask *them* what it is!"

"And give them a chance to destroy the evidence?" Ursula asked with raised eyebrows. "I think *not*. This calls for an independent investigation."

She reached for an empty plastic bag on the table.

"Wash that thing off and put it in here," she said. "I'll see if I can find out what it is."

✳ ✳ ✳ ✳

After school at Homework Club, we told Anika and Blitz the whole story.

Homework Club has pretty much become the unofficial Spy Five meeting place. Anika has to stay after school anyway because she waits for her brother Jamal to pick her up, so she stops by Homework Club sometimes to check in.

Blitz has to stay after school a lot to make up tests and other stuff he missed from being late or absent. And Ursula is willing to be there from time to time, when she doesn't have some kind of lesson or practice to go to.

And of course, Julian and I got roped into it at the beginning of the year, because Julian's grandmother thinks people actually do *homework* in Homework Club (yeah, *right*), and I wanted to hang out with Julian. At least the teacher, Mrs. Murdock, doesn't yell at us about talking anymore.

So anyway, at Homework Club we brought Blitz and Anika up to speed.

"I have a good magnifier you can use to examine that thing," Blitz said with a shudder. "If you want."

"Thanks," Ursula said. "But I'm taking it to a butcher for a professional opinion."

"Good plan," I said.

"If it *is* or *isn't* a chicken bone, a butcher will know," Ursula said.

"I sure *hope* it's a chicken bone," Anika said. "I've *eaten* those nuggets before."

"So have I," I said.

Everyone agreed, except Ursula.

"Not me. They'd have to *pay* me to eat that stuff," Ursula said. "Big bucks."

CHAPTER 2
FOWL AS FOWL CAN BE

That night for dinner, my mother brought home, of all things, chicken. Chicken kabob sandwiches, to be exact. I just couldn't eat mine. No way.

"But you *like* chicken kabobs," my mother protested.

"Not tonight," I said. "I just can't eat chicken. I'll throw up."

"Are you going on some kind of vegetarian kick?" she asked, gnawing into her kabob.

"No," I said, and I explained what happened at lunch.

"Are you sure that boy didn't make it up?" she asked, looking skeptical. "Because sometimes kids do that for attention."

"I'm sure," I said, feeling kind of nauseous from the chicken fumes.

"When I was your age, I knew a boy who'd stick a hair in his hamburger so he could get another one for free," she said.

GROSS! A hairy hamburger!

"Clarence definitely was NOT trying to get more nuggets," I said. "Can I go? I feel sick."

Even though we were sitting in front of the TV, I still felt like I had to ask to be excused from the "table," like I did in my old house.

"Sure, honey," Mom said. "I just hope you're not starving."

"I'll go get some pizza if I'm hungry later," I said.

"Hope you don't find any hairs in it," she joked.

It was *not* funny.

✳ ✳ ✳ ✳

The next morning at school, I saw Ursula in the hallway looking *very* serious.

"Did you identify the UHO?" I asked.

"Yes," she said gravely.

"What *is* it?" I asked.

She shook her head.

"I'll fill you in later," she said. "Meet me after lunch on the playground."

She started to walk away, but then she quickly turned around.

"Spencer," she said. "I would *not* eat cafeteria food at lunch today if I were you."

"Don't worry," I said. "I brought a bag lunch."

"Good," she said. "I don't want anyone puking at my presentation."

"*Presentation?*" I asked, but she was already heading off down the hall.

✳ ✳ ✳ ✳

Ursula wasn't kidding about the presentation. After lunch she was out on the playground, standing next to a big diagram of a chicken skeleton she'd taped up to the fence.

I gathered around with Blitz, Anika, Julian, Clarence, and a couple of other kids as Ursula started to explain.

"The butcher identified the UHO as a piece of a chicken neck vertebra," Ursula said, pointing to the neck on her skeleton diagram.

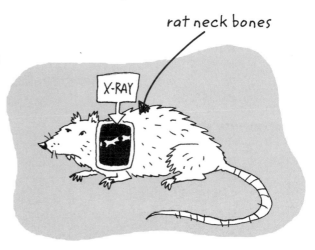

rat neck bones

X-RAY

"Aw!" one kid said. "I thought it was gonna be a *rat's* neck."

"*I* thought it was gonna be some kind of *pigeon* part!" another kid said. "Like a beak!"

pigeon beak

foot

"Or a foot!" someone else said.

"It's *still* gross, people!" Clarence bellowed. "We're eating chicken necks!"

"Yeah," someone said. "That's *disgusting.*"

"Chicken neck meat is just as edible as any other chicken meat," Ursula said. "But unfortunately, the nuggets aren't really made of chicken *meat.*"

The crowd gasped.

"What *are* they made of?" Julian asked.

Ursula pulled down the chicken poster to reveal a picture of a pile of...weird globby stuff.

Everyone looked at the poster like this:

People called out all kinds of guesses, trying to figure out what the stuff was.

"GUM?"   "WORMS?"
"SLUGS?"   "JELLYFISH?"
"DIRT?"   "TRASH?"

"No!" Ursula said. "It's fat and skin!"

"*Whose* fat and skin?" Clarence asked.

"CHICKEN fat and skin," Ursula said, looking pretty exasperated.

"That's supposed to be a picture of fat and skin?" someone asked. "It looks like a pile of..."

"Will you *please*!" Ursula said. "This is serious. They're feeding you *fat* and *skin*!"

Everyone looked kind of confused.

"It *looks* like meat," someone said.

"It *tastes* like meat," someone else added.

"It's *supposed* to look and taste like meat," Ursula said. "That's the *trick*! But really it's mashed-up skin and fat, plus lots of chemicals and other junk."

"How do you know?" Clarence asked.

"The butcher *said*," Ursula insisted.

"How does *he* know?"

"'Cause he *knows*!" Ursula said. "He's a butcher!"

"Then why was there a *neck bone* in my nugget?" Clarence demanded. "If it's all fat and skin, then how did a neck bone get in there?"

"Yeah!" someone else said.

"I don't know," Ursula said. "I'm just telling you what the butcher told *me*!"

"That's really gross," someone said quietly. "*If it's true.*"

"It *is* true," Ursula said, looking kind of dejected.

The crowd was getting smaller and smaller every second. People were drifting off to talk or chase each other around like usual.

"Tough crowd," I said, walking up to Ursula.

"I can't believe they don't care if their food is fake!" Ursula said.

"You tried," Blitz said with a shrug. "They just don't want to think about it."

"*I* for one am not gonna eat that stuff anymore," Anika said. "Not another nugget."

"Yeah," I said. "Me neither."

"Thanks guys," Ursula said, looking very serious. "But I'm not giving up yet. Just wait...."

CHAPTER 3
THIS MEANS WAR!

The next day at lunch, Ursula came up to me and Julian and announced her plan.

"I know what my presentation was missing," she said.

"Another chicken picture?" Julian asked.

"No," Ursula said with a scowl. "*Proof*. Hard evidence. So I've decided to get the list of ingredients in those nuggets."

"How?" I asked.

"I'm just going to go in there and read the label," she said, pointing to the kitchen.

"Past all those cafeteria ladies?" I asked.

"Good luck," Julian said. "They're fierce."

"*Please*," Ursula said. "It's just a simple matter of reading a label."

"But how are you planning to get *in* there?" I asked. "They don't let kids past the counter."

"If you want, we could create a distraction," Julian interrupted. "Like spill a tray or something. Then you could run inside..."

"Or we could wait till after school when no one's around," I suggested.

Ursula looked at us like we were crazy.

"I'm just going to *ask* the cafeteria ladies if they'll show me the package," she said.

"You're gonna *talk* to them?" Julian asked in disbelief.

"It's worth a try," Ursula said.

"But they're *nasty*," Julian said.

"They're just like that 'cause people are really rude to them," Ursula said. "I'll be polite to them, and they should be polite to me. *Simple.*"

Julian and I looked at her with raised eyebrows.

"I'll go with you," I said to Ursula. "Safety in numbers."

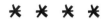

charming Ursula

So Ursula and I headed into the kitchen.

"Turn on the charm," Ursula said as we walked in there. "Big smiles."

I looked over to see if Ursula was smiling, because it was such a rare event, and she was!

Inside the kitchen, most of the cafeteria ladies were in the back, since they were almost done serving lunch. One lady was still standing at the counter, so we went right up to her. She did *not* look happy, let me tell you. Her mouth looked like it was frozen in a permanent frown.

"Um, excuse me," Ursula said. "But we were wondering if we could see the ingredients label for the chicken nuggets."

"We didn't serve nuggets today," the lady said, looking at us with very grumpy eyes.

"We're just curious for the future," Ursula said.

"Why?" she asked, looking very suspicious.

"Just 'cause," I said. "We want to know what we're eating. You know, 'You *are* what you eat.'"

The lady rolled her eyes.

permanent frown

angelic smiles

"You kids don't eat those nuggets—you just throw 'em around," she sniffed.

"I have *never* in my *life* thrown a nugget," Ursula said earnestly. "Or any of your other menu items."

"Me neither," I chimed in.

We both smiled as angelically as possible. But Grumpy Lady was not having any of it.

"Look, I'm busy right now," she said. "I can't just drop everything and go dig a bag of nuggets out of the freezer."

Somehow she didn't look very busy, standing there with her empty spatula, with no kids in line for food.

"Could we make an appointment and come back another time when you're not so busy?" Ursula asked.

Her Royal Grumpiness looked at us like we were completely insane. I have to admit, it probably sounded that way.

"Look," she said. "If you really want that kind of information, have your parents call the school."

"Don't *we* have any rights around here?" Ursula asked, sounding annoyed.

"*Rights?*" Miz Grumpy asked, suddenly looking very amused. "I don't know, honey—you'll have to check the Constitution. Now if you don't mind, I have to clean up."

So we left. Ursula was *really* fuming.

"We made a simple request," Ursula said. "And she treated us with such *disrespect.*"

"She probably thought we were really weird," I said with a shrug. "Kids don't usually care about that kind of stuff."

"That's no excuse," Ursula said, shaking her head. "This means war!"

* * * *

cough syrup juice!

We started planning "the war" that day after school.

"I think they're hiding the truth about their food," Ursula said. "That's why they didn't want us to see the label."

"I bet it's worse than just the nuggets," Anika said. "Have you ever tasted their orange juice? It's like cough medicine."

dirt cookies!

"And those chocolate cookies taste like dirt," Blitz said. "I can't believe they can actually mess up *chocolate*."

slime pizza!

"And that slimy pizza cheese," Julian said. "It's like they give us all the grossest stuff on purpose."

"I bet they save all the good stuff for themselves," I said. "And then after we're all gone, they lock all the doors and have a feast."

"Yeah!" Julian said.

We decided the only way to find out the truth about the food was to sneak into the kitchen when no one was around. We just had to find the right time to do it.

And so began **PHASE 1: CAFETERIA SURVEILLANCE.**

PHASE 1 went on for the next couple of days. Everyone took turns keeping watch at different times (between classes and before and after school) and making notes in our surveillance notebook. Here's what we found out:

CAFETERIA SURVEILLANCE

Wednesday, 7:15 a.m.

The cafeteria ladies are already in the kitchen making breakfast. How early do they get here?

Note: Couldn't get very close due to toxic odor of sausage (or something).

—Ursula

Wednesday, 2:10 p.m.

Cafeteria lady packs up crate of cookies and milk for Homework Club. Chucks it all in there and then drops crate on floor.

Note: *No wonder the cookies are always broken.*

—Julian

Wednesday, 3:00 p.m.

Cafeteria ladies are gone for the day. Kitchen all locked up.

—Anika

WEDNESDAY, 3:30 P.M.

Kitchen door propped open. Janitor inside mopping. Loud music coming out.

—Blitz

Thursday, 6:50 a.m.

Cafeteria ladies are already here making breakfast. How long does it take to heat up hash browns? I am _not_ coming any earlier than this!

Note: Maybe this is why they're so grumpy.

—Ursula

Thursday, 10:00 a.m.

Truck outside, delivery people carrying in boxes with markings like "foam trays" and "beef patties."

—Spencer

Thursday, 1:40 p.m.

Cafeteria ladies are all sitting at one of the lunch tables drinking coffee. They're on break, I guess. They say, "What do you want?" and "You're not supposed to be down here," and stuff like that. RUDE PEOPLE!

Note: What did I ever do to them?

—Anika

Thursday, 3:20 p.m.

Kitchen door open. Janitor inside again, mopping and listening to music.
—Julian

Thursday, 3:45 p.m.

Janitor still inside. Singing. Loud.

Note: I got close enough to sketch out a map of the kitchen. He didn't even notice.
—Spencer

THURSDAY, 4:00 p.m.
JANITOR'S GONE.
KITCHEN DOOR
LOCKED.
—BLITZ

Friday, 6:30 a.m.

Okay, so they get here at 6:30.
That's it. I'm going back home.
—Ursula

We got some pretty good information, so on Friday after school we met to discuss **PHASE 2: KITCHEN INFILTRATION.**

"Looks like we have an opportunity to sneak in there around 3:30," I said. "When the janitor's mopping and listening to music."

"And gettin' his groove on," Anika added with a smile.

"That too," I said.

"*Today?*" Julian asked, looking up at the clock. It was already almost 3:00.

"I have my clarinet lesson today," Ursula said. "Can't we infiltrate on Monday?"

"Works for me," I said.

Julian and Blitz agreed. But like always, Anika said she couldn't stay past 3:00.

"Sorry guys," she said. "But I'll help spread the word about whatever you find out."

And with that, she took off.

"I have to leave soon, too," Ursula said, looking at her watch. "Let's start planning."

So I got out my map of the cafeteria.

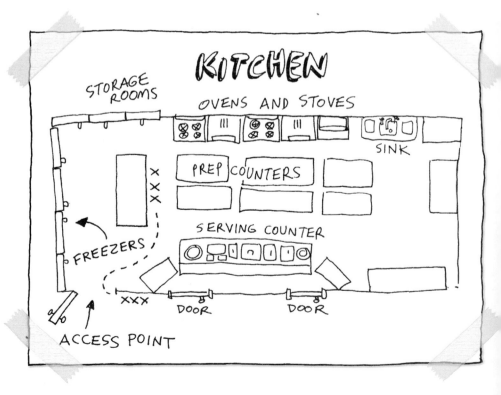

We decided it would be me, Julian, and Ursula sneaking into the kitchen, and Blitz on guard outside the cafeteria to warn us if anyone was coming.

"We'll wait right here beside the kitchen door till we're sure the janitor's facing the other way," I said.

"I'll bring a little mirror so we can look inside without sticking our heads in."

"Cool!" Julian said.

"Then we can hide behind the counters somewhere around here," I continued, "because he always mops this side first. Then we just have to wait for him to leave."

See the janitor in the mirror?

"What if he locks the door behind him?" Julian asked.

"I checked the lock," Blitz said. "It's a dead bolt you can open from inside."

"Perfect," I said.

dead-bolt lock

light switches

"And the light switches are here," Blitz said, pointing to the corner next to the door. "The janitor turns 'em off when he leaves."

"Good to know," I said.

"I have a flashlight you can use to find your way to the switches," Blitz said. "I'll bring it Monday."

"We'll need a camera, too," Ursula said. "So we can take pictures of the label and stuff."

"No problem. I'll bring you one that can take good close-ups," Blitz said.

"Anything else we need?" I asked Blitz.

"Yeah," Blitz said. "A lot of luck so you don't get caught. This could look *really* bad."

He did have a point there.

I looked over at Ursula, but she didn't even blink.

"That's why we'll be *really* careful," Ursula said, grabbing her bag and slinging it over her shoulder. "See you guys on Monday."

She started to walk off, but then she quickly turned around.

"Oh," she said. "One more thing. I think we should all wear gray on Monday, to blend in with the kitchen decor. You know, *camouflage*."

camouflage
outfits

"Gray? Who has gray *pants*?" Julian demanded.

"Well, at least wear a gray *sweatshirt*," she said. "And jeans."

After Ursula left, Julian turned to me.

"Man, that girl is *bossy*," he said.

"No kidding," I said. "But she's right about the gray, I think."

"What if she's all bossy like that in the kitchen?" Julian asked with a wince.

I shrugged.

"Hopefully we won't be talking that much in the kitchen," I said.

"I'm gonna wear *red*, just to see the look on her face," Julian said, then thought about it for a second. "Just kidding."

So on Monday at 3:25, we were all set, decked out in kitchen-colored clothes with our infiltration gear in hand.

- ☑ Camera
- ☑ Flashlight
- ☑ Pocket mirror
- ☑ Notebook
- ☑ Pencil
- ☑ Backup pencil

We went quietly down the stairs to the cafeteria, and Blitz took his position beside the stairwell, where he could watch for approaching janitors, teachers, and other problems.

Then Julian, Ursula, and I snuck around the corner into the cafeteria. Sure enough, the kitchen door was propped open, and music was coming out, exactly according to plan.

"Perfect," Ursula whispered.

We crept up to the kitchen door and stood on one side of it while I held out a mirror to make sure the janitor was facing the other way. It was pretty intense—my heart felt like it was on turbo drive.

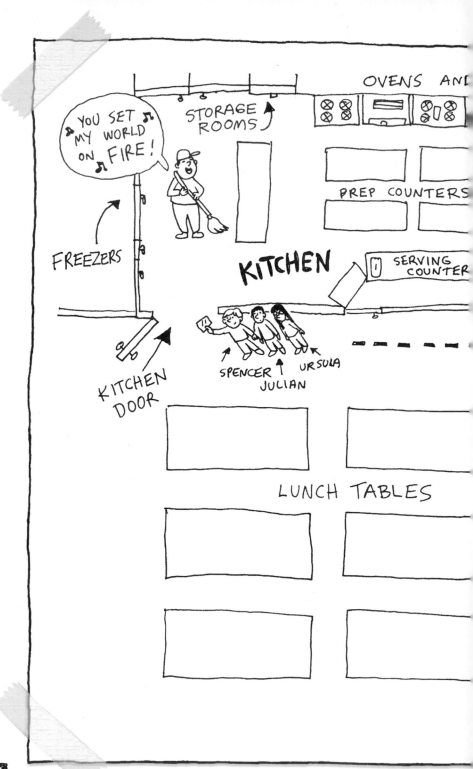

STOVES

SINK

KITCHEN INFILTRATION

MONDAY
3:30 P.M.

BLITZ

STAIRWELL DOORS

When I gave the okay signal, we crept through the door and ducked behind the counters on the side that was already mopped.

Then it was just a matter of waiting.

And waiting.

And waiting.

And then FINALLY the radio went off and the janitor wheeled his mop and bucket out of the kitchen, closing the door behind him. We heard his key turn in the lock.

"YEAH!" Julian said, sort of quietly, but not *really* quietly.

"Shhh!" Ursula said immediately.

I could tell Julian didn't like that too much. But before he could say anything, I quickly changed the subject.

"It's weird that the janitor didn't turn off the lights," I said.

"Maybe he doesn't always do that," Ursula shrugged.

"Blitz *said* he did," Julian said.

But Ursula wasn't paying any attention. She was already heading toward the freezers.

"Let's not waste any time," she said, lifting the big silver handle on one of the freezers and pulling open the door.

A big blast of cold air came out.

"AHHH!" Julian said. "That's nice."

"Don't just stand there," Ursula said, rummaging through the bags in the freezer. "Check the other freezers."

"*Geeeez*, calm down," Julian said.

Julian gave me an "I-told-you-she'd-be-like-this" look, and I gave him an "I-know-but-what-can-we-really-do-about-it-now" look. Then we each went over and pulled open a freezer of our own. Mine had lots of peas and carrots, but no nuggets.

"This thing is full of Tater Tots," Julian said. "I don't see any nuggets."

"Jackpot!" Ursula said, holding up a huge white bag labeled CHICKEN NUGGETS.

Julian and I both rushed over.

"The butcher said that if it doesn't say 'all white meat' or 'rib meat,' then it's just mashed up fat and skin and meat particles," she said. "AND LOOK!"

She pointed to the label. Sure enough, it didn't say "all white meat." It said stuff like "chicken flavoring" and "chicken powder" (yech!), and there were lots of other chemical-sounding words. Ursula was almost cackling with joy.

"Yay!" she said. "I was right!"

"Ursula," I said. "This is not a good thing. This is a *gross* thing."

INGREDIENTS: chicken, water, egg white solids, gelatin, chicken powder, milk solids, salt, partially hydrogenated soybean and/or cottonseed oil, maltodextrin, chicken fat, hydrolized corn protein, soy protein isolate, sodium phosphates, guar gum, dextrose, chicken flavoring, soy flour, mono and diglycerides, sodium alginate, monocalcium phosphate, oleoresin, paprika, annatto extract.

"Oh, right," she said. "Sorry. I forgot you guys *eat* these things."

"*Ate*," I said.

"Quick," she said, handing the bag to me. "Hold the bag up so I can snap a picture of the label."

Julian and I stood on either side of the bag and held it up.

"Pull the bag straight so it's not wrinkled," she said. "Now angle it toward me. No...there's a glare on it now...more toward me...okay, now hold it steady..."

"*Geez!*" Julian said. "Will you hurry up and take the picture?"

"Stop moving!" Ursula said. "Do you want it to be blurry?"

"I'M *NOT* MOVING!" Julian said, very loud.

Both Ursula and I looked at Julian in shock.

"*WHAT?!*" he demanded.

"Stop talking so loud," Ursula said. "Someone's gonna..."

"WILL YOU STOP BOSSING PEOPLE AROUND?" Julian shouted.

"Look, Julian," Ursula said. "I know there's a lot of pressure, but if you can't take the heat, you should stay out of the..."

And that's when Julian went...

Okay, so things were not going very well at that point. But just when I thought they couldn't get any worse, I heard...

"Excuse me!"

It was a woman's voice, coming from the back of the kitchen. We all immediately turned to see...

A CAFETERIA LADY!

We all froze.

"Hand over that bag of nuggets *right now*," she said, sounding very serious.

I immediately gave her the bag.

"We weren't trying to steal them," I said.

"We were gonna put them right back," Julian said.

"A *likely* story," she said. "I know what's going on here."

I suddenly had this vision of myself in the principal's office...then in handcuffs getting carted off by the police...then having to face the wrath of Mom. I was so wrapped up in all that, I couldn't even begin to explain the real story. Fortunately Ursula stepped forward.

"Please let me explain," Ursula said. "We're here because I wanted to know the ingredients in the chicken nuggets. I tried to ask one of the ladies at the counter, but she just laughed at me. So I took matters into my own hands. That's all there is to it."

She paused for a moment, then pointed at me and Julian and added:

"They were just helping me. They shouldn't get in trouble."

Wow, that was nice. I looked at Julian to see if he agreed, but he didn't look back. I guess he wasn't ready to think anything good about Ursula.

"So..." the cafeteria lady said slowly. "I finally get to meet the girl who wanted to know about the chicken nuggets."

And then, amazingly, the lady's frown turned into a smile!
Whoa!

Ursula immediately brightened up.

"You *know*?"

"Yes," the lady nodded. "I'm Marge Yardley, the cafeteria manager. And you are...?"

We all introduced ourselves, and Marge told us we could call her Marge instead of being all formal. Then she explained how she'd heard about Ursula and her nugget quest.

"I was very disappointed when I heard Linda say she didn't show you the label," Marge said. "I asked her to point you out so I could show you myself. But then she never saw you in the lunch line after that."

"Oh," Ursula said. "That's because I always bring my lunch from home."

"Then why are you so concerned about the nuggets?" Marge asked, looking confused.

"It's a public service," Ursula said. "I think kids should know what they're eating. And the ingredients in these nuggets are pretty...yech."

Marge looked very sad.

"I completely agree with you," she sighed. "But we have a strict budget, and we have to make do with that. A lot of the better-quality stuff is just too pricey."

"But what if we found ways to save money, or *earn* money?" Ursula suggested.

"I'm trying," Marge said. "Believe me, I'm trying. It's just very hard to run a cafeteria, especially a crazy one like this."

I could only imagine.

"So much is wasted with all the food fights," Marge continued. "And then we have problems with theft, too."

"Someone steals your food?" Julian asked in disbelief.

"I'm afraid so," Marge said. "Someone's been taking boxes of chocolate pudding for quite some time. That's what I thought *you* were here for, actually. I thought I'd *finally* caught my pudding thief."

"The thief only steals *pudding?*" I asked.

"Yes," Marge said. "It's very strange. Whenever an order comes in, at least one box of pudding goes missing. We just had a big order come in last week, so these past few days I've been staying late to see if I can catch the thief in the act."

"So you just sit here and wait in the kitchen?" I asked, wondering why we'd never seen her.

"No, I sit in my office in the back," she said, pointing in the general direction of her office, which of course we hadn't even realized was there.

pudding
thief

"Do you have any suspects?" I asked.

"Nope," Marge said. "The person is extremely quiet, that's all I can say. Because a couple of times the pudding went missing while I was sitting right there in my office!"

"Wow," Julian said.

"I guess I can't hear very well back there," Marge said. "But I certainly heard *you*."

Ursula and I looked at Julian, who looked like he was embarrassed and annoyed at the same time.

"Anyway," Marge said with a wink. "You're clearly not the pudding thieves, so I won't toss you in the slammer...but Ursula, if you have any more questions about the food, please come see me anytime."

"Thanks," Ursula said. "I will."

"But wait!" I said, as Marge started ushering us to the door. "We can help you catch the pudding thief!"

"Yeah!" Ursula said.

"Oh, that's okay," Marge said. "I can handle this myself. It's not appropriate for kids to be involved."

"Please," I said. "It'd be a great way for us to learn...stuff."

I was grasping at straws.

"Yeah, let us help," Ursula said. "Please?"

"Well," Marge said. "If you *really* want to help..."

"YES!" we all said in unison.

"I'll think about it," Marge said.

As we walked out of the kitchen, I felt this surge of energy, thinking about us catching the pudding thief.

But then I looked over at Julian scowling at Ursula, and I could see storm clouds ahead. Big ones.

CHAPTER 5
THE SPY FOUR

As we walked away from the kitchen, Julian stayed on the other side of me from Ursula and talked to me like she wasn't there.

trouble brewing

"I think Ursula should be fired from the Spy Five," Julian said. "We can be the Spy *Four*."

"Hey!" Ursula shot back. "I'm not the one who had the meltdown!"

"*You're* the one who was bossing everyone around!" Julian said.

"I was just telling you what to do!" Ursula said.

"EXACTLY!" Julian bellowed.

Then we saw Blitz poking his head around the corner.

"Could you guys be ANY louder?" he asked.

"Oh, don't worry," Ursula said. "Julian already exploded and we got busted."

"It was NOT my fault!" Julian insisted.

I could tell he was getting ready to blow again. I'd never seen Julian act so...volcanoey. It was weird.

"You got *caught*?!" Blitz said.

"Don't worry, we're *not* in trouble," I said. "And it was actually *good* that we got caught."

"WHAT?" Blitz asked, totally confused.

storm clouds

So I told him the whole story, all the way up to the part about the pudding thief.

"Cool!" Blitz said. "I have the *perfect* gadget to catch a thief in the act. I just finished my first prototype, actually. Come back to my place and I'll show you."

✳ ✳ ✳ ✳

As we walked to Blitz's place, Ursula cornered me while Julian was talking to Blitz.

"I think *Julian* should be fired from the Spy Five," Ursula said. "He completely blew the infiltration."

I winced, because of course Julian heard.

"*You're* the problem!" Julian said. "You were like, '*Do this, do that!*' Wasn't she, Spencer?"

Great. Caught in the middle.

Fortunately I didn't have to say anything because Ursula burst right in there with:

"You're just a *misogynist!*"

All of us gasped.

"A *what?*" Julian asked.

"A MISS-ODGE-IN-IST," Ursula pronounced. "It means you hate girls."

"That *is* NOT true," Julian said.

"If it were Spencer telling you what to do, you wouldn't care," Ursula said. "But because it's *me*, and I'm a girl, you get mad."

"Spencer doesn't boss me around," Julian said. "Right, Spencer?"

Caught in the middle!

I took a deep breath.

"Listen, guys," I said. "Let's not argue anymore."

"Then fire Ursula," Julian said. "And no one will argue."

"Fire JULIAN!" Ursula shot back. "*He's* the LOUDMOUTH!"

"Look," I said, taking another deep breath. "Ursula, maybe you could say stuff like, 'Will you hold this?' instead of 'Hold this.'"

"What's the big difference?" Ursula asked.

"I don't know—it just sounds less..." I said.

"*Bossy*," Julian said.

Ursula glared at both of us.

"So you're on *his* side?" Ursula asked me.

Cornered again!

"Can't we just move on?" I asked, totally despairing. "Can't we talk about the pudding thief? Or the weather? Or *something*?"

"Yeah," Blitz said. "This is getting really old."

"I'm going home," Ursula announced, immediately turning around and walking the other way.

"Good riddance," Julian said under his breath.

But I'm sure Ursula heard.

GOOD RIDDANCE

"**D**oes this mean Ursula quit?" Julian asked as we walked up the stairs to Blitz's place.

fruit flies all over Blitz's room

"I don't know," I said, trying not to make a big deal out of it. "I think she's just mad."

"What was that word she called Julian?" Blitz asked. "A mirage-onist?"

I gave Blitz a four-alarm "what-are-you-thinking" look. The last thing we needed was to start the whole thing up again.

"Who cares," I said.

"Yeah, she probably made that word up," Julian said.

Somehow I wouldn't bet on that. But *anyway.*

Blitz's room was a mess, like usual, but this time it had swarms of fruit flies in it. They were all whizzing around when we opened the door.

"I think there's a banana in here somewhere," Blitz said. "My mom keeps trying to get me to eat them for breakfast."

There was definitely a rotten-banana-y smell in the air.

"I think I should invent a food detector," Blitz said. "Like a metal detector, but it would find lost food."

"Or you could just get a dog," Julian suggested.

"Good point," Blitz said.

Blitz went right over to his workbench and picked up a little gray box.

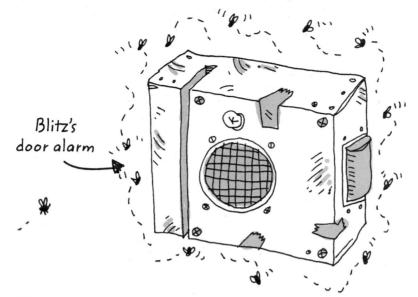

Blitz's door alarm

"This is my latest invention," he said. "It's a door alarm."

"Oh, yeah," Julian said. "You showed us that before. But you weren't done yet."

"Well, now it's done," Blitz said. "Lemme show you."

We followed Blitz outside his room. He closed the door and attached the alarm on the outside, right above the doorknob.

"I designed this so I'd know if my sister was trying to get into my room while I was out there watching TV," he said, pointing to the living room.

"You have a sister?" I asked, looking around for a sign of her.

"Yeah," he said. "Sarah. She's four. She's at day care right now. Otherwise she'd be trying to get in here. She loves going through my stuff. It's really annoying."

"Why don't you just put a lock on the door?" Julian asked.

"I used to have a chain lock on the outside that she couldn't reach, but now that Sarah's bigger, that doesn't work anymore. She just opens it."

"What about a *key lock?*" Julian asked.

Cool card swipe entry
for the alarm

"My mom won't let me install one 'cause she's afraid *I'll* lose the key or *she'll* lose the key or I'll lock myself in there and then the building'll burn down—I don't know, she's kind of paranoid," Blitz said. "But this system is perfect. It has a key entry, too."

Blitz showed us a little card with a ridge in it.

"Card swipe entry," he said, sliding the card down the slit on the side of the alarm. The alarm made a clicking sound and a little light came on.

"Sweet!" Julian said.

"Wait till you see what happens when you open the door," Blitz said with a smile. "Go ahead, try it."

So Julian opened the door.

"Cool!" we both said.

"And see how the light goes off now?" Blitz said. "That lets me know if my sister went in my room while I wasn't here."

"What if it was your mom or... someone else?" I asked. I wasn't sure if Blitz's parents were divorced or not.

"I gave my parents their own keys," Blitz said. "So if the alarm gets set off while I'm gone, I'll *know* it was my sister, and she'll get in BIG trouble. It's perfect. She's completely neutralized."

Blitz's little sister

"Nice," Julian said.

"It's for her own good," Blitz said. "There's a lot of stuff in here she shouldn't be touching."

"So how could we use this thing to catch the pudding thief?" I asked, changing the subject.

"Well, the pudding's in a storage room, right?" Blitz said. "We can rig this up on the storage room door, and Marge'll be able to hear the alarm in her office when the thief goes for the pudding."

"Excellent," I said.

"But *we* want to be there to catch the thief, too," Julian said.

"Well, I guess we could wait with Marge," Blitz said. "But who knows when the thief'll strike? That could be a *lot* of waiting."

"I'd do it," Julian volunteered.

"Maybe we can make it happen faster," I said. "I have an idea...."

CHAPTER 7
CHOCOLATE PUDDING VIBES

That night at home, I asked my mom if I could buy some chocolate pudding packs at the store.

chocolate fever

"Sure," she said, handing me a ten. "And get me some chocolate ice cream while you're at it."

Just as I thought—chocolate fever is contagious!

The next morning before school, I gave two chocolate pudding cups to Julian.

the pudding thief

mmm mmm!

"Whoa," he joked when he saw my supply. "Are *you* the pudding thief?"

"This is the *bait* to lure the thief," I explained. "I figure it's someone who works here or goes to school here, right? So if we all eat chocolate pudding and carry it around school, maybe we'll stir up the thief's cravings."

"Good plan," Julian said. "Especially if it means I get to eat chocolate pudding."

Just then, Anika came running in.

"What happened? What happened?" she asked excitedly. "Did the infiltration go okay?"

So we told her the story (skipping the part about Julian's meltdown and Ursula's storm-off), all the way up to my plan with the chocolate pudding bait.

the janitor, the leading suspect

"Great idea, Spencer," she said. "We'll get some chocolate pudding vibes in the air...I like it."

And then she thought for a second.

"You know who I suspect?" she asked.

"*The janitor*," Julian and I said together.

"Exactly," Anika said. "We should definitely make sure *he* gets the pudding vibes."

And with that, Anika took her two pudding cups and grabbed her backpack from the floor.

"I'll see you guys at lunch, then," she said.

For the rest of homeroom, I kept my eye on the door to see if Ursula would show up.

But she didn't.

✳ ✳ ✳ ✳

That day at lunch, Julian and I ate our chocolate pudding and made sure plenty of people knew it. We gave some pudding to Blitz, too, and he helped spread the vibes. I looked for Ursula, but I didn't see her.

"Is Ursula absent today?" I asked Blitz.

"No, she's here," Blitz said. "She was in my reading class. She looked kind of grumpy, but then she *always* looks like that."

After lunch, Julian, Blitz, and I hung out on the playground, looking at Blitz's alarm, which he'd brought to show Marge. We were talking about our plan to set it up for her after school when Anika came up to us.

"Well," she said. "The janitor's ruled out."

"Why?" I asked.

"I offered him one of my pudding cups, and he said, 'No thanks, I'm lactose intolerant.'"

"What does *that* mean?" Julian asked.

"It means he farts when he eats stuff with milk in it," Blitz explained. "My dad does that."

"*Okay*...thanks for sharing," Anika said.

Can't eat pudding!

"Anytime," Blitz said.

"So now we have *no* suspects?" Julian asked.

"Well, the janitor could be taking the pudding for someone *else* to eat," I said.

"Good point," Anika said. "And we haven't ruled out all the cafeteria ladies, either."

"No," I said. "But we can ask Marge about all that after school."

"Ursula's in there talking to her right now," Anika said. "She told me she had an *appointment.*"

"*Really?!*" we all said at once.

Anika nodded.

"Aw! She's trying to crack the case before *us!*" Julian said.

"I thought we were all in this together," Anika said, looking concerned.

"We *are,*" I said. "It's just we sort of had a fight..."

"I know," Anika said, looking at Julian. "She told me. But it's over now, right?"

"Not if she's gonna boss people around and call people *names,*" Julian said with a shrug.

"I know she can be a little bossy," Anika said. "But she's not trying to disrespect you. She's just trying to get stuff done. Give her a chance."

Julian shrugged again.

Ugh. Would this *ever* blow over?

Will the Spy Five survive?

THE SPY FIVE

* * * *

That day when Julian and I got to math class, Ursula was already there, sitting at her desk on the other side of the room, reading a book on her lap.

Since people are actually acting civilized in math class these days, there was no chance for me to sneak over and talk to her. But I kept an eye on her, and she actually managed to read the *entire*

Ursula reading during math class?

class, keeping the book out of view under her desk. Miss Pryor didn't even notice.

Ursula still reading?

And then, after class, Ursula walked out of the room *still* reading! I chased after her.

"Ursula!" I called.

"What?" she asked flatly.

"Sorry about yesterday," I said. "Julian definitely overreacted."

"I know," she said casually. "But you know what? Yesterday you told me the second habit of highly effective managers."

"*What?*" I asked, completely confused.

Then she showed me the cover of her book. It was called *The Eleven Habits of Highly Effective Managers*.

"Have you ever read this?" she asked.

"Um, no..." I said.

A book like that would not exactly be at the top of my reading list (if I *had* a reading list).

"It's very interesting," she said. "Marge gave it to me."

"What's the second habit?" I asked.

She opened to the second chapter.

interesting reading ?

"Like you said," she explained. "You're supposed to *ask* people to do things, not *tell* them. Even though you're *really* telling them, you have to *pretend* like you're asking. People really hate being told what to do."

"You *don't* say," I said.

"It's true," Ursula said. "They like to think they have a choice. It's human nature. People are very..."

But she couldn't finish, because she was interrupted by the obnoxious sound of:

"GO TO CLASS!
GET OUT OF THE HALLS!"

"Ugh," Ursula groaned.

"*He* needs to read that book," I said.

"No kidding," Ursula said.

Mr. Naulty, ineffective principal

So, happily, the Spy Five was *not* coming apart at the seams after all.

That day after school, Julian and Ursula were both at our meeting, and they actually even apologized. Well, sort of.

After the "apologies" were over, we talked about the pudding business.

"There was definitely a pudding buzz by the end of the day," Anika reported.

"I know the teachers noticed," Blitz said. "My first pudding got taken away 'cause I was eating it during science, and the second one got taken during silent reading."

"Mr. Naulty blasted me for eating mine in the hall," Julian said. "And *lots* of people heard him, of course."

"So hopefully the pudding thief is primed for action," I said.

"I hope he makes his move *today*," Julian said.

"Who says it's a *he*?" Ursula pointed out.

"Ugh," Julian said, rolling his eyes. "Okay, I hope HE or SHE makes HIS or HER move today."

"Did Marge give you any good leads at your meeting?" I asked Ursula.

"Oh, we didn't talk about the *pudding thief*," Ursula said. "We talked about revamping the lunch menu."

"Really?" I said. "We can *do* that?"

"Sure," Ursula said. "They waste a lot of money on food kids won't eat. And on junky nuggets, too."

Julian's food pick: chocolate chip cookies every day!

"Hey, I know!" Anika said. "Let's do a survey! We can pass out forms to the whole school, and kids can fill in the stuff they want for lunch."

"That's a good idea, actually," Ursula said. "Very democratic."

"Yeah," Julian said. "I'll vote for chocolate pudding and real chocolate chip cookies every day."

"I second that," Blitz said.

"But what about vegetables and stuff like that?" Ursula asked. "Marge says they have to serve vegetables no matter what."

"I'll vote for guacamole," Julian said.

GUACAMOLE

Julian's veggie pick: guacamole every day!

Blitz's veggie pick: curly fries and ketchup!

"I'll vote for curly fries and ketchup!" Blitz said. "*Two* vegetables!"

Blitz and Julian slapped each other five.

"I can see our survey results are gonna be very...interesting," Anika said with a smile.

✳ ✳ ✳ ✳

A little later we all went downstairs to show Blitz's alarm to Marge. We set it up on the storage room door, way up high so the thief wouldn't spot it. Then we gave Marge a demo.

"What a clever invention!" she said.

"So you'll use it?" Blitz asked, looking proud.

"Sure," Marge said. "Looks like it'll be very helpful. After two years, I'm getting a little tired of wondering who this pudding prowler is."

"It's been going on for *two* years?" I asked.

"Sure has," she said.

up high to keep it out of sight

KEEP OUT

"And you're sure it's not anyone who works in the kitchen?" Anika asked.

"Oh, *no*," Marge said. "I trust my staff. And besides, only one of them has been here the whole time this has been going on, and I *know* she'd never do such a thing. Linda—you remember her."

"Ugh," Ursula said. "*She's* the one who was rude to us."

Linda, the RUDE cafeteria lady

"They're *all* rude," Julian said.

"I'm sorry about that," Marge said. "But you know, they're all just really tired of the nonsense that goes on at lunch. They work so hard cooking food and then it gets treated with such disrespect. They get no appreciation."

She shook her head sadly.

"Maybe we can work something out," I said. "Like if kids promise not to throw food around, they get to pick stuff they really like for the lunch menu."

"Yeah," Ursula said. "A reward system!"

"I'd be *really* impressed if you could make *that* happen," Marge said.

"It's worth a try," Anika said, checking her watch. "Sorry, guys, but it's 3:00 and I gotta bounce."

"See ya," we said as she took off.

"Don't you *all* have someplace you're supposed to be?" Marge asked. "Don't you have homework to do?"

"No way," Julian said. "We want to be *here* to catch the pudding thief."

"Yeah," Blitz said. "I want to see my alarm in action!"

"Who says the thief's going to strike *today*?" Marge asked.

"Can't we just wait and see?" I asked.

"We can talk more about the lunch menu while we're waiting," Ursula suggested. "We have more ideas."

"Well, *all right*," Marge said. "Just this once."

"Shouldn't we go hide out in your office so we won't scare him OR HER away?" Julian asked, eyeing Ursula.

"*All* of you?" Marge asked.

"Yeah!" we all said.

So we all went to Marge's office and squeezed in. There was only one chair in there, so everyone but Marge sat on the floor.

A few minutes after we settled in, we heard the janitor's music filtering down the hallway from the kitchen.

SUDDENLY..... LIFE HAS NEW MEANING.... ...TO MEEEEEEEEEE!

NUTRITION NOTES

"Kelvin's here," Marge said with a smile. "He mops the floor every day for me."

"Are you sure it's not *him*?" I asked.

"Oh, I trust Kelvin," Marge said. "I've even asked him to keep an eye out for anything suspicious, but he's never seen anything. I think it happens after he's gone, anyway."

"Then wouldn't the person need the key to the kitchen?" I asked. "Who has the key?"

"Oh, *lots* of people have that key," she said. "Some of the science teachers keep things in the cold storage room, and all of the building service and security people have the key. The list is just too long. I'm sure I'll be very surprised by whoever it is. Now, weren't we going to talk about the lunch menu?"

So while Kelvin mopped, we told Marge about the lunch food survey idea. She liked it a lot, and she even helped us come up with some survey questions. She also let us look through her

French bread pizzas

YUM!

cheese-and-bacon potato skins

food catalogs, and we were all practically drooling looking over things like French bread pizzas, cheese-and-bacon potato skins, and chicken fingers.

"All white meat!" Ursula said, pointing to the description of the chicken fingers. "Not like those nasty nuggets. Marge, can't you order these instead?

"They're expensive," Marge said. "We don't have enough budget for that. I wish we could just..."

And that's when we heard it:

KEEP OUT!
KEEP OUT!

And we quickly ran out into the kitchen to find...

YUM!

YUM!

YUM!

chicken fingers

KEEP OUT! KEEP OUT!

Kelvin, the janitor, caught by the pudding-thief trap!

"Kelvin!" Marge said, once the alarm finally went quiet. "*What* are you doing?"

"Sorry!" he said. "I saw this little contraption on the door, and I was just curious what it did."

"You were caught by our pudding-thief trap!" Marge said.

Kelvin looked horrified.

"Oh, no! I hope you don't think it's me," Kelvin said. "Really, I don't even touch the stuff, 'cause I'm..."

"...*lactose intolerant*," Blitz, Julian, and I said along with Kelvin.

Marge, Ursula, and Kelvin looked at us like we were crazy.

"How did you *know*?" the three of them asked at once.

"We heard," I said with a smile. "You told our friend Anika."

"Oh," Kelvin said, looking pretty embarrassed. "Well, really, I don't steal..."

"Of course I trust you, Kelvin," Marge said. "We should have warned you. These kids are helping me catch the thief. They installed this alarm today."

Then she pointed at Blitz and added, "It's his invention."

"Very clever!" Kelvin said.

"They're hoping to make a catch today," Marge said.

"Well, good luck," Kelvin said. "I've been keeping an eye out for a *year*, and I've never seen a thing."

And then suddenly his eyes got really wide. He pointed at the open kitchen door.

"I just heard the stairwell door slam!" he said in a loud whisper. "Someone's coming!"

"Duck!" I said.

DUCK! *Someone's coming!*

We all ducked down behind the counters as the footsteps got nearer and nearer.

And then, to our surprise, through the doorway stepped...

ANIKA AND HER BROTHER!

Blitz, Ursula, Julian, and I immediately jumped up when we saw who it was. And of course, that REALLY took Anika and Jamal by surprise.

"*You guys!*" Anika said. "You almost gave me a heart attack!"

"Yeah," Jamal said. "I think you just took ten years off my life!"

After Anika caught her breath, she introduced her brother.

"Everyone, this is my brother Jamal," she said. "I told him about the pudding thief and how I really wanted to come back and check out what was going on, and he said okay."

"Little did I know..." Jamal said.

"Oh, come on," Anika said. "Can we show him the alarm?"

"Sure," I said. "But first let's close the door so the thief doesn't get scared away."

So we closed and locked the door, and then Blitz showed Jamal how the alarm worked. He was pretty impressed.

And that's when I thought of something.

"You know," I said. "Maybe it would be better to put the alarm down *low*, since Kelvin spotted it when it was up high."

"Great idea," Blitz said, removing the alarm and sticking it way down low on the door.

Blitz adjusting the alarm

But just as Blitz was setting up the alarm, Anika suddenly whispered:

"Keys! I hear keys!"

And sure enough, there were jingling keys outside the door!

"Duck!" I whispered.

"But the alarm isn't rigged!" Blitz protested.

"Too late!" I said.

And we all ducked behind the counters again. This time it was a real CROWD of us.

While we all practically held our breath, the key turned in the lock, and the door slowly opened.

It was hard to see from where I was crouched, so I couldn't tell who it was at first. I just heard footsteps moving across the kitchen to the storage room.

Julian was the first to see who it was. His eyes went all enormous like this:

Anika was the second to see, and her eyes got all enormous, too.

Then Blitz:

Then Marge and Ursula:

I could hardly stand the suspense!

Then I heard the storage room door swing open, and I leaned out a little farther to see who it was...

It was MR. NAULTY! I couldn't believe it! What would Mr. Naulty want with a box of pudding?

And more importantly—what were *we* going to do about it?

I looked at Marge for help. *I* certainly didn't want to be the one who jumped up and yelled "Stop, thief!" to Mr. *Naulty* of all people! That could be completely fatal.

MR. NAULTY!
IS THE PUDDING THIEF!!!

CHOCOLATE
PUDDING

And then, just as Mr. Naulty was heading out with the box, Marge motioned for all of us to stay quiet and keep low. Then she stood up and walked out into the kitchen behind him.

"Bill," she said, calling Mr. Naulty by his first name.

Mr. Naulty caught red-handed!

MAN! Did *he* jump!

Then Mr. Naulty turned around, looking stunned.

"Where are you going with that box?" Marge asked calmly.

"This?" he asked, as if there was *another* box. "Oh, this is for the...office."

Marge looked him dead in the eye.

"Bill, I don't have enough budget to keep this cafeteria stocked with decent food," she said. "We *definitely* can't afford to have boxes of pudding disappear."

Mr. Naulty looked flustered.

"Yes, um..." he said. "That *is* a problem."

"A *big* problem," Marge said.

"Well," Mr. Naulty began, setting the box of pudding down on the counter, "I'll just leave this here, then."

"Thanks," Marge said. "Have a good night."

GUILTY!!

Mr. Naulty looking embarrassed

And with that, Mr. Naulty slinked out the door.

"OH, MAN!" Julian said when the coast was clear. "This school is so MESSED UP! The principal is a CRIMINAL!"

"I can't believe it!" Kelvin said in shock.

"*Believe it,*" Anika said, shaking her head.

"What a slimebag," Blitz said.

"MARGE! Aren't you going to *press charges*?" Ursula demanded. "Or *something*?"

"Oh, there's no need to involve the police," Marge said.

BUT MARGE, IT'S THE PRINCIPLE OF THE MATTER. AND IT'S THE PRINCIPAL!!!

"BUT MARGE!" Ursula protested. "You have to! It's the *principle* of the matter. And it's the *principal!*"

"Yeah!" Julian said. "He should rot in jail!"

"People don't usually go to jail for trying to steal pudding," Jamal pointed out.

"Well, he should at least get *handcuffed*," Julian said. "And fingerprinted."

"He's a repeat offender," Ursula added. "That would count against him a *lot* in a court of law."

"Wow," Marge said. "You really want to let him have it, huh?"

"YES!" we all said at once.

"Well, don't worry," Marge said. "The teachers and staff at this school are getting pretty fed up with Mr. Naulty's nonsense, and we're keeping an eye on him. We'll keep records of stuff like

Mr. Naulty in handcuffs

Mr. Naulty on trial

this, and when the time comes, we'll file a nice big report with the district office."

"Will he get the ax?" Blitz asked excitedly.

"I don't know," Marge said. "We'll have to see."

"Come on," Ursula said. "Can't you file the report *now*?"

"Yeah! Kick his sorry butt out on the street!" Julian said.

"I'm afraid it's going to take a little more than a pudding problem for *that* to happen," Marge said.

"But Marge, it's the principle..." Ursula started to protest again.

"*Anyway*," Marge said, changing the subject. "The important thing right now is that the pudding mystery is solved, and I have *you all* to thank for that!"

"Yeah, great job, guys!" Kelvin said. "I'm impressed!"

"And *now* that we won't be losing boxes of pudding anymore, we're one step closer to affording better-quality food," Marge added. "Every little bit counts! So let's keep working on your lunch food survey, because *that* could be a huge help, I think..."

And then Marge went on and on about how we could save *more* money for the good stuff by cutting a little bit here and a little bit there, and wasting less, and all that business.

But I, for one, was not really listening. *My* mind was busy enjoying one very delicious thought: Mr. Naulty caught, exposed, humiliated, cornered. Ha! Serves him right.

empty
pudding cups

CHAPTER 9
SMOOTHIE THINGS OVER

So I guess we'll just have to wait and see what happens when Marge and the other teachers file their big report on Mr. No-Good Naulty. In the meantime, maybe we can dig up some more dirt on him to help out.

I'm still not exactly sure why Mr. Naulty wanted the pudding. Marge said some people just really *really* like chocolate...and have snack attacks...and are too cheap to buy their own pudding...*and* are sneaky and shifty enough to take stuff that's not theirs. So I guess Mr. Naulty is one of those people. *Yech.*

Anyway, the whole crazy story spread really fast around school, thanks to Anika's big network of friends. Good thing

Anika has a solid reputation for true gossip, because otherwise I don't think anyone would've believed it.

no yelling?

I wonder if Mr. Naulty realized everyone knew, because for some reason, he hasn't been storming around the halls these days. Hopefully that's a permanent change. But I wouldn't bet on it.

The other good thing is that we *did* do the lunch food survey we were talking about. Marge helped us make up the survey forms, and we got help from Miss Pryor and a couple of other teachers who let kids fill out the surveys in class.

The teachers *also* got kids to sign statements saying that if they got better food and the chance to have some say in the menu, they wouldn't throw stuff around anymore.

PLEASE WRITE AND SIGN THIS STATEMENT:

I promise not to throw any kind of lunch food, drink, plate, utensil, or condiment.

_____
your signature here

Miss Pryor

The surveys looked like this:

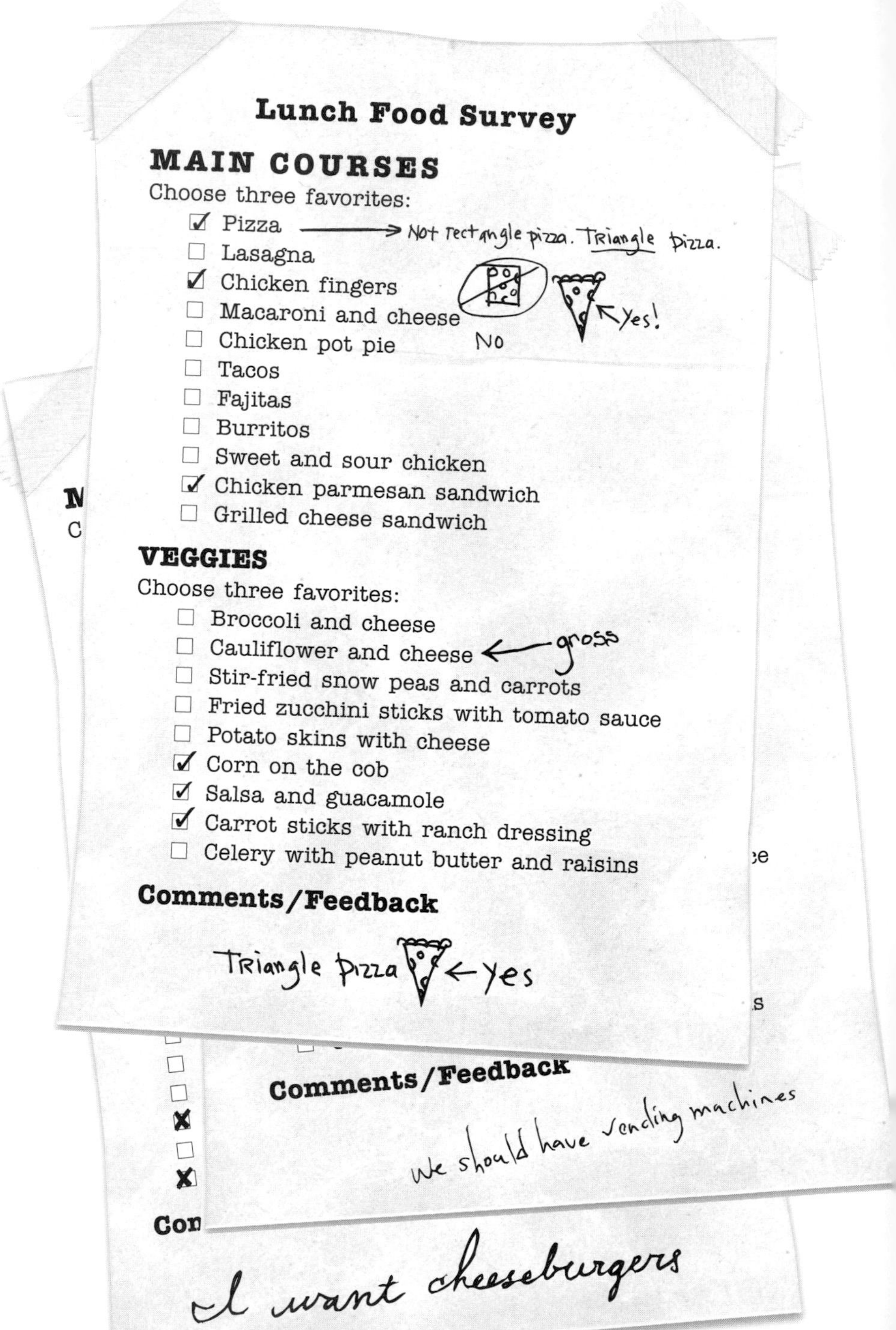

Lunch Food Survey

MAIN COURSES

Choose three favorites:

- ☑ Pizza ——→ Not rectangle pizza. <u>Triangle</u> pizza.
- ☐ Lasagna
- ☑ Chicken fingers
- ☐ Macaroni and cheese   No
- ☐ Chicken pot pie
- ☐ Tacos
- ☐ Fajitas
- ☐ Burritos
- ☐ Sweet and sour chicken
- ☑ Chicken parmesan sandwich
- ☐ Grilled cheese sandwich

← Yes!

VEGGIES

Choose three favorites:

- ☐ Broccoli and cheese
- ☐ Cauliflower and cheese ←— gross
- ☐ Stir-fried snow peas and carrots
- ☐ Fried zucchini sticks with tomato sauce
- ☐ Potato skins with cheese
- ☑ Corn on the cob
- ☑ Salsa and guacamole
- ☑ Carrot sticks with ranch dressing
- ☐ Celery with peanut butter and raisins

Comments/Feedback

Triangle pizza ← yes

Comments/Feedback

We should have vending machines

Con

I want cheeseburgers

Lunch Food Survey

MAIN COURSES
Choose three favorites:
- ☐ Pizza
- ☒ Lasagna
- ☐ Chicken fingers
- ☒ Macaroni and cheese
- ☐ Chicken pot pie ◁—YUCK
- ☐ Tacos
- ☐ Fajitas
- ☒ Burritos
- ☐ Sweet and sour chicken
- ☐ Chicken parmesan sandwich
- ☐ Grilled cheese sandwich

VEGGIES
Choose three favorites:
- ☒ Broccoli and cheese ◁— *make sure there's lots of cheese!*
- ☐ Cauliflower and cheese
- ☐ Stir-fried snow peas and carrots
- ☒ Fried zucchini sticks with tomato sauce
- ☐ Potato skins with cheese
- ☐ Corn on the cob
- ☐ Salsa and guacamole
- ☒ Carrot sticks with ranch dressing
- ☐ Celery with peanut butter and raisins

Comments/Feedback

Less veggies, more fries please!

(overlapping sheet, left)

MAIN
Choose thr
- ☐ Piz
- ☒ Las
- ☐ Chi
- ☒ Ma
- ☐ Chi
- ☐ Tac
- ☐ Fa
- ☒ Bu
- ☐ Sv
- ☐ Ch
- ☐ G

VEGGI
Choose t
- ☐ B
- ☐ C
- ☒ S
- ☒ F
- ☐
- ☐
- ☐
- ☒
- ☐

Com

Can we have strawberry milk?

(overlapping sheet, bottom)

...y with peanut butter and raisins

Comments/Feedback

How come there aren't any dessert choices?

After the results were in, we helped Marge figure out the new lunch menu. To make room in the budget for the good stuff, we got rid of A LOT of things kids weren't eating anyway, like soggy fish patties, gooey turkey casserole, stinky beef stew, clunky dinner rolls, and those scary chicken nuggets. I'm sure everyone will be sorry to see all *that* stuff go (ha ha ha).

Marge posted the results on the kitchen door, and people got all excited and crowded around to check it out. The new menu just kicked in this week...

chicken fingers:
top choice
main course!

pizza:
second place
main course!

potato skins
with cheese:
top veggie choice!

corn on the cob:
second place
veggie choice!

...and believe it or not, lunch has actually looked like this for the past couple of days:

But at least for now it's good, because the people who *didn't* like flying food are happy. I heard this girl Marisol from my silent reading class talking about it the other day.

Marisol from silent reading

And of course, Clarence and his crew are glad they don't have to be on the lookout for UHOs anymore.

Ursula *also* came up with the idea of having a fruit smoothie stand on Fridays, because Marge told her that lots of fruit was going to waste at the end of the week.

It's been a real hit.

WELCOME TO, URSULA'S Smoothie STAND

The profits go toward buying _more_ good lunch food!

Ursula even gave the first smoothie to Julian, to "smoothie things over" once and for all.

5

I think it kind of worked.

So, anyway, that about wraps up the story of our cafeteria quest. I never would have imagined that Clarence's UHO would take us on such a crazy trip. But I guess that's what happens when you go to a school where so much is messed up. Who knows what's next for the Spy Five...can't wait to find out.

Until then,

Spencer

P.S. Ursula saw my notebook, and she says, for the record, that she doesn't look anything like the way I draw her.

And I am not grumpy.

P.P.S. Anika also saw my notebook, and she says she doesn't wear clothes like the ones I draw her in.

My pants are not too short.

P.P.P.S. Give me a break, people!

Spy Gear Manual

DOOR ALARM

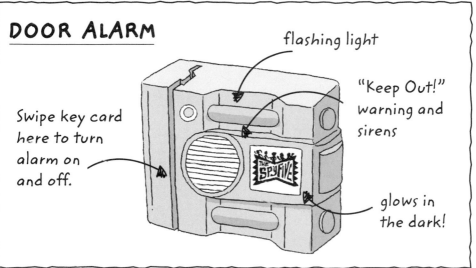

flashing light

"Keep Out!" warning and sirens

Swipe key card here to turn alarm on and off.

glows in the dark!

Key Cards:

They glow in the dark!

Access Option #1:
Hide your second key card somewhere outside your room in case you lose the first one.

Access Option #2:
Give your spare key card to a friend, or anyone who has clearance to enter your room.

HOW TO USE YOUR DOOR ALARM WHILE YOU'RE OUT...

<u>Gotcha!</u>

If you're going to be near your room, you'll be able to hear the sirens, so you can catch snoops in the act!

<u>Someone Was Here...</u>

If you come home and find the alarm light no longer flashing, then someone entered your room while you were out! Now you just have to figure out whodunnit....

<u>Whodunnit?</u>

If you have a smooth floor outside (or in) your room, try sprinkling a thin layer of baby powder on the floor right in front of your door. Can you see footprints? Do the prints match any of your suspects' shoes?

Alarming Idea #1:
Put your door alarm down low on your door so people won't realize it's there.

Alarming Idea #2:
Disconnect the wires to the speaker, so your alarm will be silent. Then you'll be able to see if intruders entered, but you won't alert them that they've been detected!

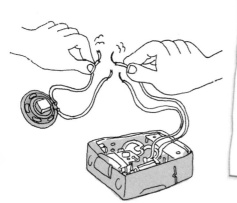

...AND WHILE YOU'RE IN THE ROOM

Intruder Alert!
If you put your alarm on the <u>inside</u> of your door, you'll be alerted the moment intruders barge in! Then you can put away any secret stuff.

MORE THAN A DOOR ALARM!

Desk Guard

You can also rig up your alarm to guard something important on your desk. Just place the alarm next to the object and make sure the object presses up against the door alarm's trigger button. If someone touches the object or tries to move the alarm, the alarm will go off, and you'll know when you get back that your stuff was touched!

Drawer Alarm

Your alarm will also work with some drawers and closets. Just make sure there's something to press up against the alarm's trigger button.

However you set up your alarm, snoops are going to be sorry they barged in on YOU!

Good luck catching 'em red-handed!
— Spencer